Summary, Analysis & Review

of

Stephanie Dray's and Laura Kamoie's

America's First Daughter

A Novel

by Instaread

Please Note

This is a summary with analysis.

Copyright © 2016 by Instaread. All rights reserved worldwide. No part of this publication may be reproduced or transmitted in any form without the prior written consent of the publisher.

Limit of Liability/Disclaimer of Warranty: The publisher and author make no representations or warranties with respect to the accuracy or completeness of these contents and disclaim all warranties such as warranties of fitness for a particular purpose. The author or publisher is not liable for any damages whatsoever. The fact that an individual or organization is referred to in this document as a citation or source of information does not imply that the author or publisher endorses the information that the individual or organization provided. This concise summary is unofficial and is not authorized, approved, licensed, or endorsed by the original book's author or publisher.

Table of Contents

Summary 4

Main Characters 11

Analysis 14

Character Analysis 14

Relationships 17

Themes 20

Authors' Style 25

References 28

Instaread on America's First Daughter

Summary

America's First Daughter by Stephanie Dray and Laura Kamoie is the story of Martha "Patsy" Jefferson Randolph, a daughter of Thomas Jefferson. Based on Jefferson's letters and actual historical events, the novel imagines Patsy's struggles to remain loyal to her father while following her own heart during America's turbulent post-Revolutionary years.

The novel opens in 1826 just after the death of Jefferson. Patsy is left to go through her father's letters. In addition to Patsy, Jefferson is survived by Sally Hemings, a slave about Patsy's age who is the half-sister of Jefferson's late wife. Hemings was his lover for many years and the mother of several of his children. Patsy knows the story of her father's long relationship with Sally can never be told. It is Patsy's duty to protect both her father and her country by keeping his secrets.

In Part One, "The Dutiful Daughter," Patsy recalls the time a frantic messenger arrived at Monticello, Jefferson's Virginia plantation, to warn Jefferson that the British were coming. The year is 1781. Patsy is only eight years old. Jefferson loads his wife, Martha, along with Patsy and her younger sister Polly, into a carriage. He entrusts them to his 22-year-old friend William Short and promises to catch up with them later.

Jefferson avoids capture by the British, then takes his family into the mountains to hide. William shows up several weeks later to report that the British are retreating, thanks to the intervention of the Marquis de Lafayette. Then Lafayette tells Jefferson that his American countrymen want him to represent the United States in Paris. But Martha doesn't want Jefferson to go.

Less than a year later, back at Monticello, Martha dies after giving birth to her third daughter, Lucy. But first, she asks Patsy to promise that she will always look out for her father. She makes Jefferson promise that he won't remarry.

Afterward, Jefferson plunges into a deep depression. Patsy remains at his side. When the Revolutionary War ends, Jefferson decides to go to Paris after all. He leaves Polly and Lucy with their aunt and, in 1784, takes 11-year-old Patsy with him. In Paris, Patsy's life is transformed. William soon joins them to serve as Jefferson's secretary.

Jefferson and Patsy receive word that baby Lucy has died of illness. So Jefferson sends for Polly. Meanwhile, Jefferson is named minister to France, replacing Benjamin Franklin.

Revolution is in the air in Paris. The peasants are increasingly intolerant of the indifferent and extravagant

French monarchy. When Jefferson leaves Paris to travel, he trusts William to look after Patsy. She becomes infatuated with William and starts adopting his abolitionist views.

In 1787, nine-year-old Polly arrives in Paris. Patsy is 15. On Christmas Day, William joins Patsy and Polly outside for a snowball fight. He chases Patsy and they collapse in the snow together. It marks the beginning of their romance.

Later that day, Patsy goes to Jefferson's sitting room and spies him kissing Sally. William sees that Patsy is upset and confronts her. He tells her she's old enough to know about relations between men and women. Patsy insists that her father's actions are sinful.

William and Patsy start spending more time together, but Jefferson refuses to grant William permission to marry Patsy. He believes both William and Patsy require more life experience. Moreover, he wants his daughter to marry Tom Randolph, the son of his longtime friend Colonel Randolph, a wealthy plantation owner.

The political conflict in Paris escalates. People's representatives start gathering in public places. Rabble-rousers make pronouncements from atop café tables. The army abandons the king.

Jefferson concedes to Patsy that he will let her marry William if William returns to Virginia. But William tells Patsy that he will not be returning; he cannot tolerate living in a slave state. He asks Patsy to stay in Europe with him. Patsy realizes that she must choose between her father and her beloved.

By mid-1798, the Bastille has fallen and many thousands of civilians are marching in the streets of Paris. By now, Sally is pregnant with Jefferson's child. Patsy declares to William that she must return to Virginia with her family for the time being, and that if William loves her, he will wait for her. William refuses to commit and the two say a painful goodbye. Because Sally is pregnant, she and her brother James return to Virginia with the Jeffersons, foregoing their opportunity to remain in France and be free.

Back in Virginia, Patsy, now 17, sees 21-year-old Tom Randolph for the first time since childhood. He is immediately enamored of her, and Patsy finds his desire a welcome distraction from her heartbreak. Jefferson gives his blessing for their marriage; he thinks Tom's family wealth and status will mean an easy life for Patsy.

But upon marrying Tom, Patsy's life is thrown into turmoil. She must deal with Tom's heartless, hateful father, the Colonel, and scandalous sisters Nancy and Judith. While they are visiting the Randolphs at their Tuckahoe plantation, Sally's baby, fathered by Jefferson, dies after the Colonel refuses to help the sick child of a slave. Not long after, Patsy and Tom learn that Patsy is expecting her first child.

In Part Two, "Founding Mother," Tom receives word that his father is dying. He and Patsy are at Monticello at the time, so he isn't able to get to the Colonel before he dies. Soon Tom learns that because he had not chosen to live closer to his father, the Colonel wrote him out of his will, which leaves his entire estate to his late wife's son instead. Tom and Patsy are left to inherit nothing but the Colonel's debts.

In 1796, Jefferson loses the presidential race to John Adams. But because he came in second in the Electoral College, Jefferson is named vice president. Jefferson doesn't share Adams's political views, including Adams's decision to ally with Britain instead of the new French republic. Jefferson decides to run against Adams the next time around. In 1800, he wins the presidency.

Meanwhile, Patsy and Tom struggle. Patsy conceives child after child, most of whom are girls, which adds to the difficulty of their lives as failing plantation farmers. In despair over the death of his parents, his lost inheritance, and a failed first bid for Congress, Tom starts drinking. He becomes abusive to Patsy and the children.

Around this time, William Short returns to Virginia. Patsy sees him for the first time in 13 years. He tells Patsy he wants to lease land he owns in Virginia to both white and black men as a social "experiment."

In office, Jefferson must battle his political nemeses along with the tabloids. Word gets out that he is the father of Sally's children. William leaves Virginia to go help Jefferson. Patsy keeps having more babies. Polly, however, becomes sick after giving birth to her third child and dies. In 1804, Jefferson is re-elected president.

In Part Three, "Mistress of Monticello," Patsy and Tom start having more success with farming, but they still face many trials. Patsy becomes pregnant with what is at this point her tenth child with Tom.

In the summer of 1812, the United States declares war on Britain. Patsy's eldest son Jeff and Tom are both called up to serve. Fortunately, they both return safely, and in 1815, the United States defeats the British for a second time. Tom is elected governor of Virginia. Within a couple of years, Patsy is pregnant again.

Jefferson's eldest son by Sally, Beverly, turns 21. Long before, Jefferson had promised Sally that he would free her children when they turned 21, the age at which slaves could be freed. But Jefferson knows that if he frees Beverly and Beverly remains in Virginia, people will realize that the young man is his son. Patsy tries to convince Jefferson and Sally to send Beverly to the North, where no one will know he was a slave. Sally chooses instead to keep Beverly at Monticello as a slave.

Then Tom announces his intentions to introduce a bill that would free Virginian slaves once they reach puberty. Patsy realizes that it's time for her to take a side on the slavery issue. Virginians reject the bill. Soon after, Beverly disappears. Patsy knows her father finally set him free.

After three terms as governor, Tom returns home. Patsy decides that they must sell their land so as not to burden their son Jeff with their debts. Tom is infuriated because not owning land will mean he'll lose his right to vote. Tom withdraws from Monticello and his family, and begins to lose his sanity.

William Short returns, and he and Patsy start talking again. Both finally admit that they still have feelings for each other. William pleads with Patsy to leave Tom, but Patsy refuses. She explains that leaving her husband would disgrace her father.

Tom abruptly leaves Patsy and Monticello, much to her relief. Patsy becomes the mistress of Monticello. Lafayette, Jefferson's dear old revolutionary friend, comes to visit Monticello. The two are reunited after many years.

In 1825, Patsy and Jeff learn the extent of Jefferson's and Tom's debts. They fear they will be forced to sell Monticello. Before his death, Jefferson leaves his plantation and other assets in trust to Patsy in acknowledgment of her loyalty to him. He asks her to look after Sally when he is dead. On the Fourth of July, 1826, Jefferson dies of old age.

Patsy makes Jeff promise not to sell Sally at the auction to be held in order to pay off Jefferson's debts. In 1829, Tom dies. Before his death, he and Patsy attempt to reconcile and Patsy promises him she won't remarry. In 1829, Patsy leaves Monticello for the last time, with William, who has returned once again, at her side. Although they never marry, due to Patsy's promise to Tom, Patsy and William are finally free to have a loving romantic relationship in their later years.

Main Characters

Thomas Jefferson is the author of the Declaration of Independence and the third president of the United States.

Martha Jefferson is Thomas Jefferson's wife. She dies in 1782.

Martha "Patsy" Jefferson Randolph is Jefferson's devoted daughter.

Polly is Patsy's frail younger sister.

Sally Hemings, a slave, is Jefferson's longtime lover and mother of six children by him.

Beverly is Jefferson and Sally's eldest son.

William Short is Jefferson's loyal friend and Patsy's first love.

Tom Randolph is Patsy's husband and father of her 12 children. He eventually loses his sanity.

Colonel Randolph is Tom's malicious father.

Jeff is Patsy and Tom's eldest son.

Ann, Ellen, Cornelia, Ginny, Mary, James, Benjamin, Meriwether, Septimia, and George are Patsy and Tom's other surviving children.

The Marquis de Lafayette is Jefferson's lifelong friend and fellow revolutionary.

Thank you for purchasing this Instaread book

Download the Instaread mobile app to get unlimited text & audio summaries of bestselling books.

Visit Instaread.co to learn more.

Analysis

Character Analysis

Thomas Jefferson

Jefferson is an idealistic and pragmatic patriot. He is unrelenting in his ability to exercise foresight, sometimes at the expense of his personal relationships. Although he is a devoted family man, Jefferson knows that committing wholeheartedly to the revolution might mean having to give up even the people he holds dearest. His first commitment is to his country. This important aspect of Jefferson's character is laid bare in the opening pages of the novel when Jefferson risks leaving his family in order to monitor encroaching British troops during a critical point of the Revolutionary War.

Patsy Jefferson

Like her father, Patsy Jefferson is an idealist. As a child at her mother's deathbed, she promises to care for her father in her mother's absence. Patsy never questions her fidelity to her father. Rather, she simply understands it as a core, constitutive aspect of her identity. What defines Patsy is her resilience. Time and again she steps up to protect her family's reputation and well being, often at great personal cost.

Like her father, Patsy is inspired by the revolutionary spirit of the times. She embraces social change and aligns herself with people like William Short and Tom Randolph who model a commitment to leading the charge and ushering in social progress. Patsy has a strong moral conscience and opposes slavery. At the same time, she understands that undoing the slave system will require nothing short of the complete overturning of the plantation economy. For these reasons, Patsy hesitates to commit wholeheartedly to the abolitionist cause.

William Short

William Short is a radically forward-thinking person who is committed to moving society toward greater equality for all. One of his lifelong political commitments is to the abolitionist cause. In this sense, he is much more progressive than his mentor, Thomas Jefferson. At one point, Patsy characterizes William as stubborn. In fact, William is just a consistent person who refuses to turn his back on his convictions.

Tom Randolph

Tom struggles all his life with an inferiority complex. He is passionate in his relationships and endeavors, but easily overcome by a sense of defeat when things don't work out for him. Tom struggles to negotiate his desire for success with his personal convictions. Like William, Patsy, and many others of his generation, Tom opposes slavery.

Tom wants to leave a lasting legacy, but he continues to face disappointments and rejections from people all around him who frustrate some of his best intentions. Even Patsy ultimately chooses her father over Tom by insisting on selling Tom's land in order to pay off his debts and safeguard Jefferson's reputation. This rejection by Patsy might be the most painful for Tom, the disappointment that finally puts him over the edge of his sanity.

Relationships

Thomas Jefferson and Patsy

Patsy Jefferson's relationship with her father is the most important one in her life. From the time she is a child, Patsy wants to be indispensable to her father. And she succeeds; Patsy provides Jefferson with emotional support and helps him maintain his public image and keep his secrets over the course of decades.

Patsy identifies strongly with her father's idealism, morality, and loyalty to family. At the same time, Patsy understands the hypocrisy of her father's continued holding of slaves despite his espoused commitment to liberty. In this sense, Patsy exemplifies the increasingly progressive political views of the generations following her father's.

At various points, Patsy gives up opportunities to have love, happiness, and independence in the name of fulfilling her daughterly duties. Her greatest sacrifice is turning her back on the chance to experience life with her true love, William Short, in the name of protecting her father from what would be the scandal of her running away with William while Tom was still alive. Patsy's faithfulness to her father borders on a kind of religiosity. Her fierce fidelity to him is nothing short of a vocation.

Instaread on America's First Daughter

William Short and Patsy

What initially bonds William Short and Patsy Jefferson to each other is their shared devotion to Thomas Jefferson. As William and Patsy's relationship develops, it is Patsy's differences from her father that attract William to her, and William's differences from Jefferson that attract Patsy to him. Perhaps this is because they both continually struggle to develop their own senses of themselves as influenced by but distinct from Jefferson. This struggle proves to be a daunting one for both, given the proportions of Jefferson's personality and celebrity, as well as the extent of his political power and prowess.

As Patsy and William fall deeper in love, Patsy begins to appreciate William's radical politics and daring optimism for a freer, more equitable world. Unlike her father, William is willing to sacrifice political clout, popularity, and economic stability in order to pursue what he perceives to be an ethical life. Because he is vehemently opposed to slavery, William chooses to remain in Europe, where his political future is less certain. But by following his heart, as opposed to doing what others expect or tell him to do, William ends up achieving a successful career as a diplomat.

William appreciates Patsy's determination and spirited, fiery personality—even in the face of her father's authority—for these qualities, he calls her an "Amazon." He believes that she is strong and resilient, as opposed to simply submissive to her father. But because they are both strong and principled, neither Patsy nor William is willing to concede to the other. For this reason, they never marry, though they continue to share a complicated and loving bond for all their lives.

Patsy and Tom Randolph

As their relationship progresses, Patsy develops a deep sense of devotion to Tom. Her devotion derives from her recognition that Tom, like her, values family above all else. In this sense, Patsy and Tom are more alike than Patsy and William are. But it is Patsy and Tom's similarity—their shared sympathy for and devotion to family—that is their eventual undoing. Because they are both fiercely committed to protecting loved ones, Patsy and Tom often unquestioningly offer support and refuge to family members in need. In exchange, they are often repaid with only drama and financial hardship, as in the case of Tom's sister Nancy, who becomes mired in a lawsuit alleging that she and her lover murdered their bastard child. It is Patsy who is forced to come to Nancy's aid, lying under oath to ensure the charges are dismissed.

Because she is so devoted to family, Patsy chooses her father's and her children's legacies and futures over Tom's. Her decision is enough to drive Tom to madness. Tom cannot survive what he perceives to be Patsy's betrayal of him; their loyalty to family is what each deems unforgivable about the other.

Instaread on America's First Daughter

Themes

Gender Roles

The post-Revolutionary period is not an easy one for American women. Patsy's experiences epitomize the challenges that women faced in the late eighteenth and early nineteenth centuries. White women like Patsy experienced pressure to marry well to ensure the long-term financial security of their families. Upon marrying, white women in the American South were expected to wear multiple hats and maintain simultaneous—and sometimes impossible-to-reconcile—identities. As the mistresses of plantations, they were expected to perform labor outdoors. At the same time, they were expected still to behave as "ladies" by serving as gracious hosts and selfless mothers.

In early American society, women's bodies were not their own. Patsy, for example, is almost constantly pregnant and ends up birthing 12 children. But it was more than just their bodies that American women were forced to sacrifice in the name of family and household. Women sacrificed their personal wants, needs, and principles in order to protect their husbands and families; they were expected to feign happiness in exchange for economic security. Patsy has a complicated relationship to the gender norms of her time. She adheres to these norms while also challenging them, eventually transgressing them by becoming the mistress of Monticello after Jefferson's death.

What the novel explores in much less depth is the particular difficulty of life for slave women. While Jefferson's mistress Sally is a prominent character, much less time is spent depicting Sally's suffering and sacrifices—how she gives up the chance to remain and live freely in France, for example, because she is pregnant with Jefferson's child. This minimal attention to Sally's trials is due in part to the fact that the novel is narrated from the first-person perspective of Patsy, who would only have had a limited understanding of what life was like for Sally. That said, the novel opens with a spotlight on Sally and the fact that she was one of the two most important women in Jefferson's life. By including her in this way, the novel invites readers to be critical of narratives of Jefferson's life that omit Sally.

Sacrifice

Social change does not come easily. Revolution entails massive sacrifices, many of which individuals and societies have no way of anticipating. These are themes that *America's First Daughter* explores in depth through depictions of both the American and French Revolutions. Although some historians tend to romanticize these revolutions, the novel emphasizes how they were bloody affairs that cost many people their lives. Furthermore, they entailed widespread instability and unpredictability for civilians leading up to the wars and in the years following them. As the novel suggests, being a revolutionary means being valiantly willing to give up one's life. But it also means being willing to give up one's *way* of life—which at times can be a prospect just as difficult to fathom, let alone reckon with.

America's First Daughter explores this fact through the representation of Jefferson's internal struggle around the subject of slavery. The novel remains critical of the contradictions and hypocrisies of Jefferson's character along with his self-identification as a revolutionary. It performs its critique of Jefferson by juxtaposing his choices and beliefs with those of William Short, a younger man who radically refuses the slave economy by living abroad, and who even goes so far as to imagine an experimental society where white and black people could work on plantations side by side as tenants. At the same time, the novel sympathizes with Jefferson's situation by inviting readers to imagine whether they would have been willing to give up everything in the name of social progress had they been alive during the revolutionary period.

Oppressive Institutions

The novel's sympathies with Jefferson might be read as suggesting that the institution of slavery oppressed not only African Americans but white people, as well. As the novel shows, white plantation owners had little choice but to participate in the slave economy because it dominated life in the Southern states. The alternative was nothing short of the upending of an entire way of agrarian life in the South or selling off all assets and moving to the North. This is not to say that the novel attempts to justify chattel slavery in America. Rather, it depicts how entrenched the system was, a fact that made abolition a slow and arduous process, one that would be left to subsequent generations to see through to its end.

The novel additionally makes a subtle commentary on American culture today and its continued insistence on values such as freedom and democracy in a society where racism and discrimination persist. At one point, shortly after the turn of the nineteenth century, Tom comments to Patsy, "This country is so divided," with reference to the division between the Northern and Southern economies and cultures. [1] In this way, the novel prompts readers to contemplate the divisions that fracture American society even today—"divided" has perhaps always been the most accurate descriptor for the United States.

Equality

Through its extended meditation on the American system of chattel slavery, *America's First Daughter* questions whether the patriotic Revolutionary and post-Revolutionary periods ever truly embodied values like freedom and equality. As William reminds Patsy at one point, as long as some people are held as slaves, liberty is just an idea and an ideal—not a reality. Notably, throughout the novel, it is William—and not Patsy or Jefferson, although they are the novel's primary protagonists—who serves as a kind of moral compass.

The novel likewise explores the ways in which women were treated like second-class citizens during the period. While Patsy does eventually become prominent and powerful when she inherits Monticello, it is only through her unyielding support of her father that she comes to some power and autonomy; she receives very little recognition during her lifetime. By choosing to tell the story of Jefferson's life and work through the eyes of Patsy—largely via a focus on Patsy's personal feelings and experiences—the novel performs a feminist critique of the unfair treatment of women, not only in their own times, but by historians.

The novel remains critical of revolution and equality as ideals in and of themselves. Revolutions and revolutionary movements are always at risk of being co-opted by precisely those principles and forms of power that they often set out to abolish in the first place. To illustrate this point, the novel cites the US decision, under John Adams, to ally with the British monarchy instead of the new French republic.

Authors' Style

America's First Daughter is a meticulously researched historical novel based on letters to and from Thomas Jefferson, of which he alone wrote more than 18,000. [2] Many of the events described in the book are based on historical events. Although the novel takes liberties by imagining the thoughts and feelings of Patsy Jefferson, the narrator and protagonist, it is the novel's liberties that often bring Patsy to life for readers.

The novel is narrated in the first person. As a result, Patsy becomes a relatable figure in all of her longing, desire, and disappointment. Readers witness the maturation of Patsy's intellect and emotions over the many years of her life. In this sense, *American's First Daughter* is a Bildungsroman, or a coming of age story chronicling the development of Patsy's moral character. As a result of her life experiences, Patsy is transformed from a precocious but idealistic child to a loyal, family- and country-centered adult. Notably, the novel invites readers to imagine Patsy as an extraordinary woman but also as an ordinary person who, throughout her life, faced both successes and failures, love and heartbreak.

America's First Daughter draws on the conventions of the romance novel by depicting Patsy's tumultuous, tortured romantic relationships with both William Short and Tom Randolph. By appealing to readers' emotions, and by exploring the characters' occasional fatal flaws, the novel draws on generic conventions of tragedy and melodrama. Over the course of 500-plus pages, the protagonists of *America's First Daughter*—Patsy, Jefferson, William, and

Tom—are developed with complexity. Almost all of them are flawed, but they are sympathetic in their respective commitments to reckoning with some of the most urgent political and ethical questions of their time.

~~~~ END OF INSTAREAD ~~~~

Thank you for purchasing this Instaread book

**Download the Instaread mobile app to get
unlimited text & audio summaries
of bestselling books.**

Visit Instaread.co
to learn more.

References

1. Dray, Stephanie, and Laura Kamoie, *America's First Daughter*. New York: William Morrow, 2016, p. 372.

2. "Note to Reader," *America's First Daughter*, front matter.